PUNIDDLES

pun·id·dle (pŭn·ĭd′·l)

n. 1. A pair of photographs that suggest a literal or obvious solution in a punny way. 2. *pl.* A game using the pair of photographs to deduce the punny solution. [Source: pun, riddle]

Bruce and Brett McMillan

Photography by Bruce McMillan

Houghton Mifflin Company Boston 1982

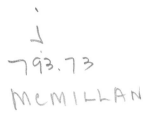

For Grammie "Winkie" and Grampa Pete

Library of Congress Cataloging in Publication Data
McMillan, Bruce
Puniddles.
Summary: Pairs of photographs of everyday sights that, when put together, take on a new and humorous meaning.
1. Rebuses. [1. Rebuses] I. McMillan, Brett, ill. II. Title.
PN6371.5.M39 779'.092'4 81-20130
ISBN 0-395-32082-8 AACR2
ISBN 0-395-32076-3 (pbk.)

Printed in the United States of America
P 10 9 8 7 6 5 4 3 2 1

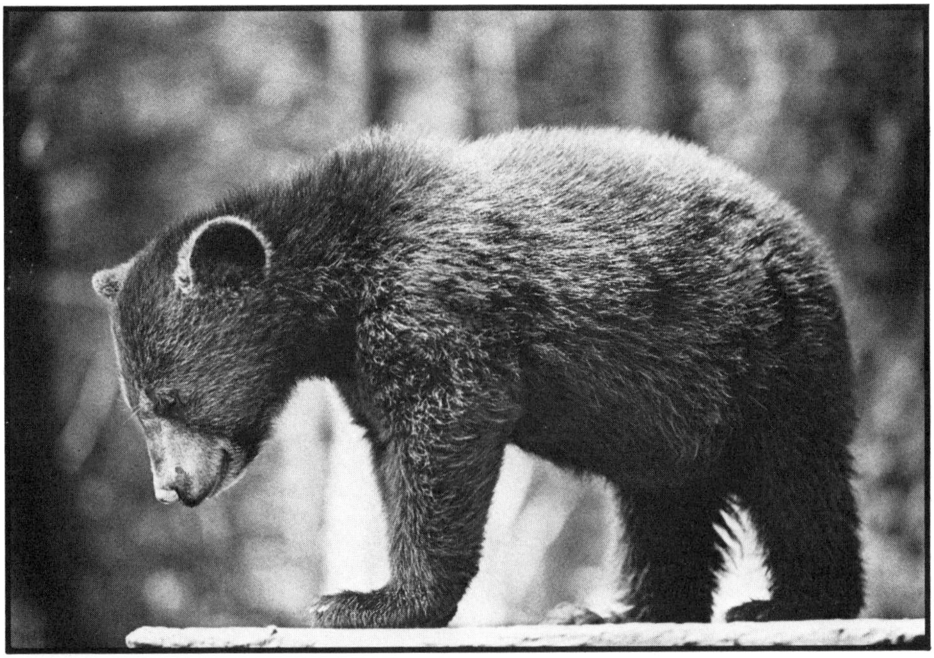

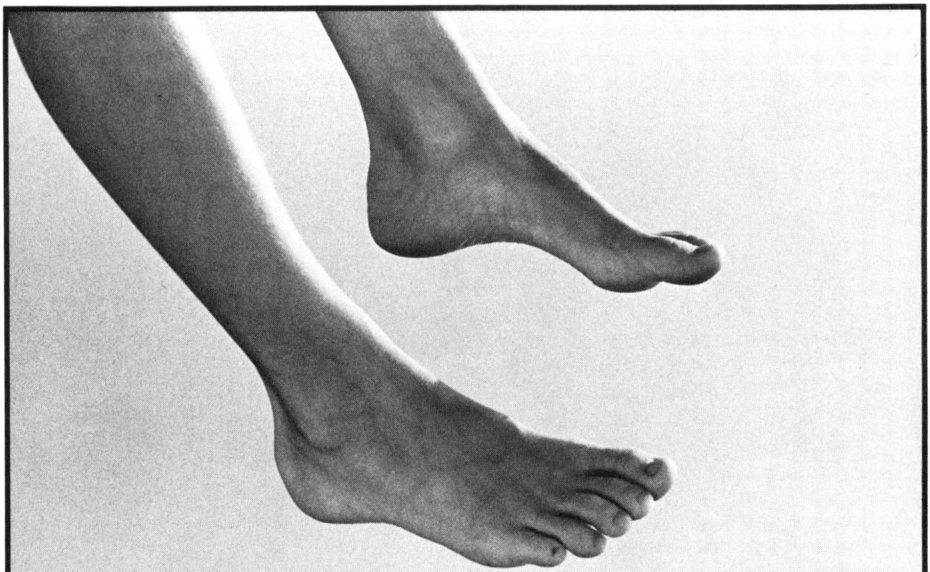

BARE FEET

HORSESHOES

COWBOYS

FIRECRACKERS

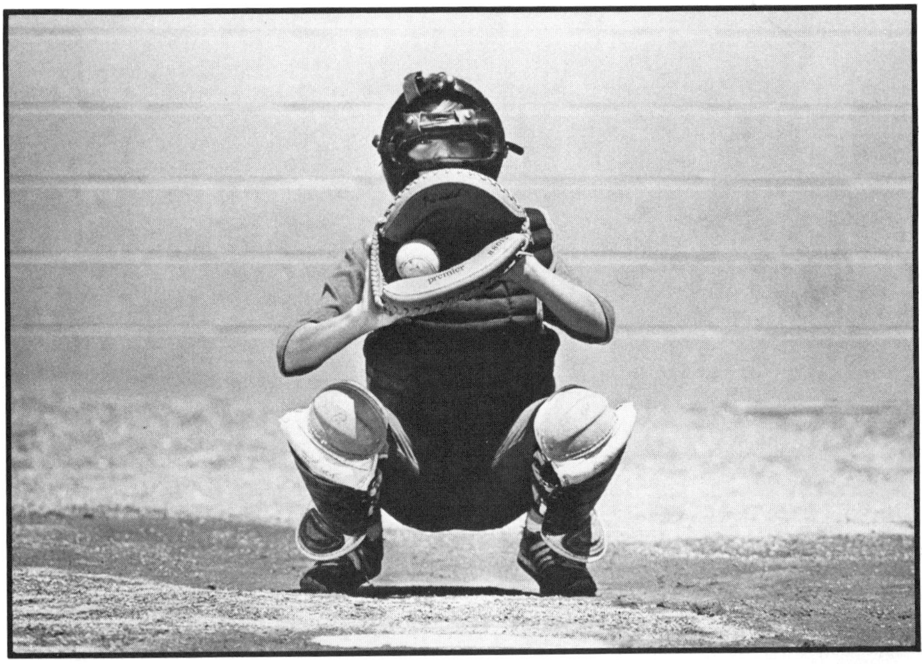

DOGCATCHER

FOUL BALL

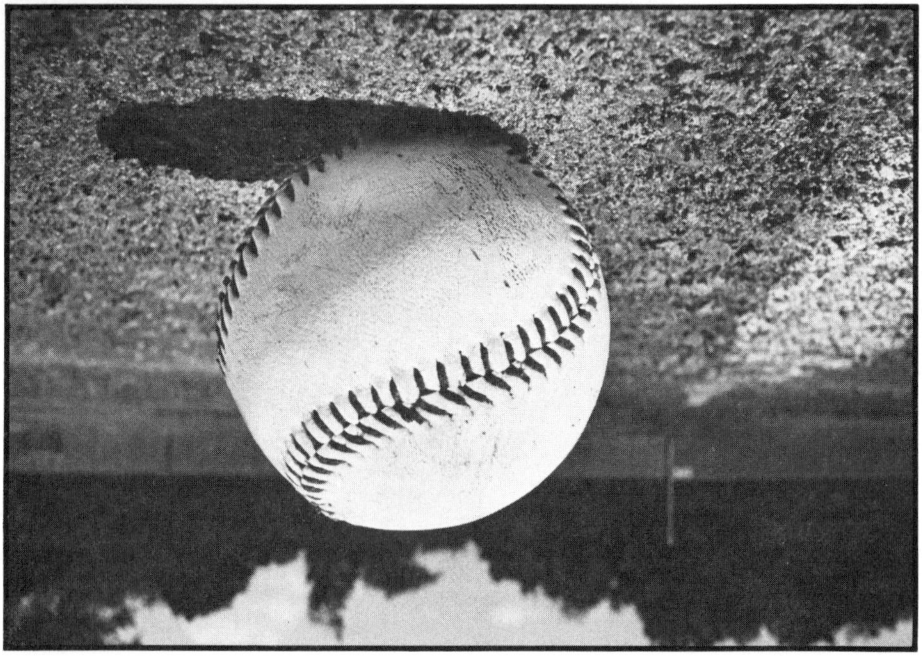

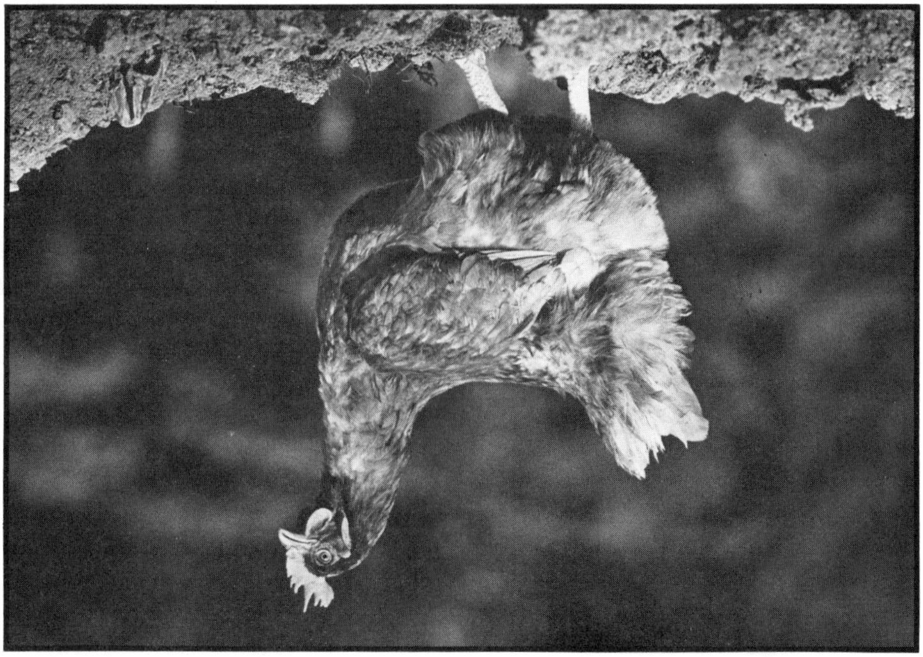

HOME RUN

RAINBOWS

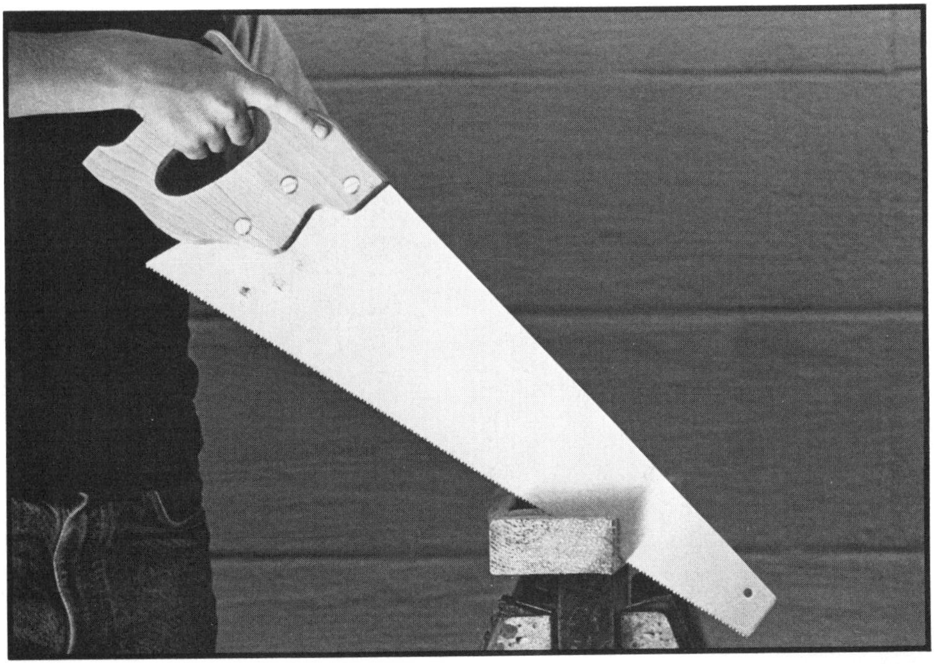

SEESAW

BOTTLE CAPS

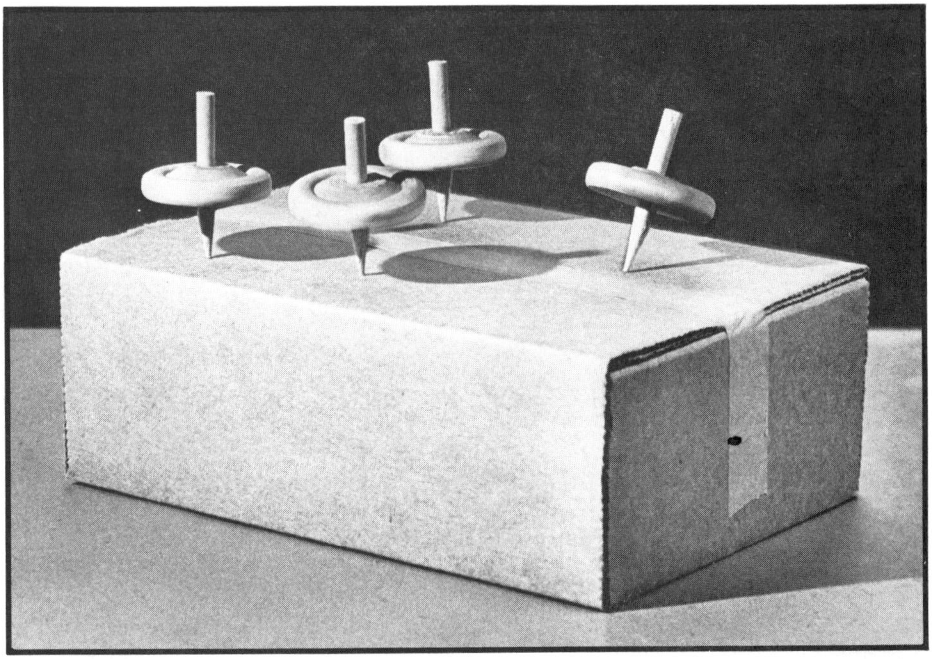

BOX TOPS

PINEAPPLES

CAULIFLOWER

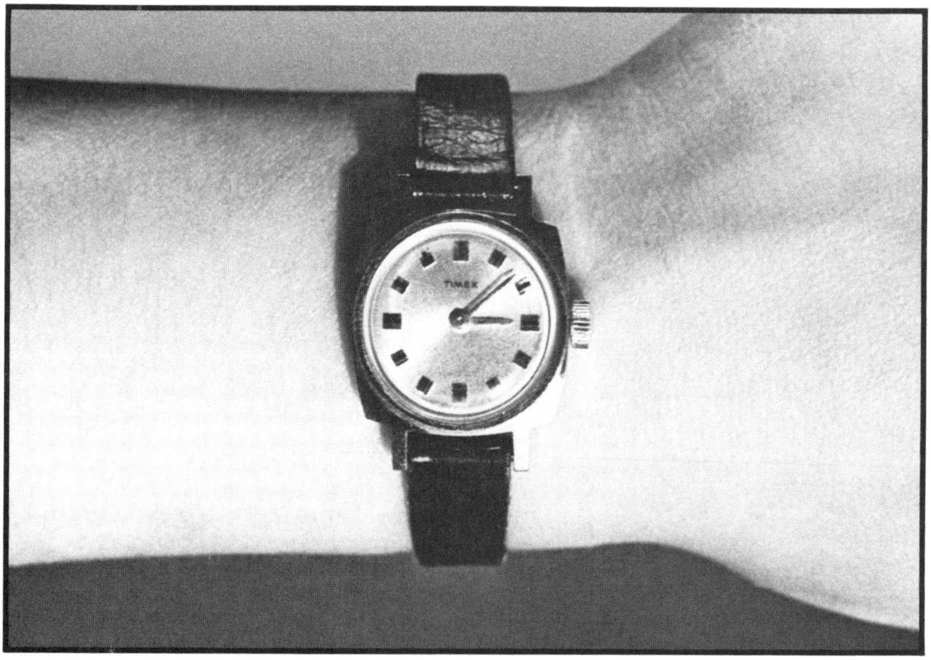

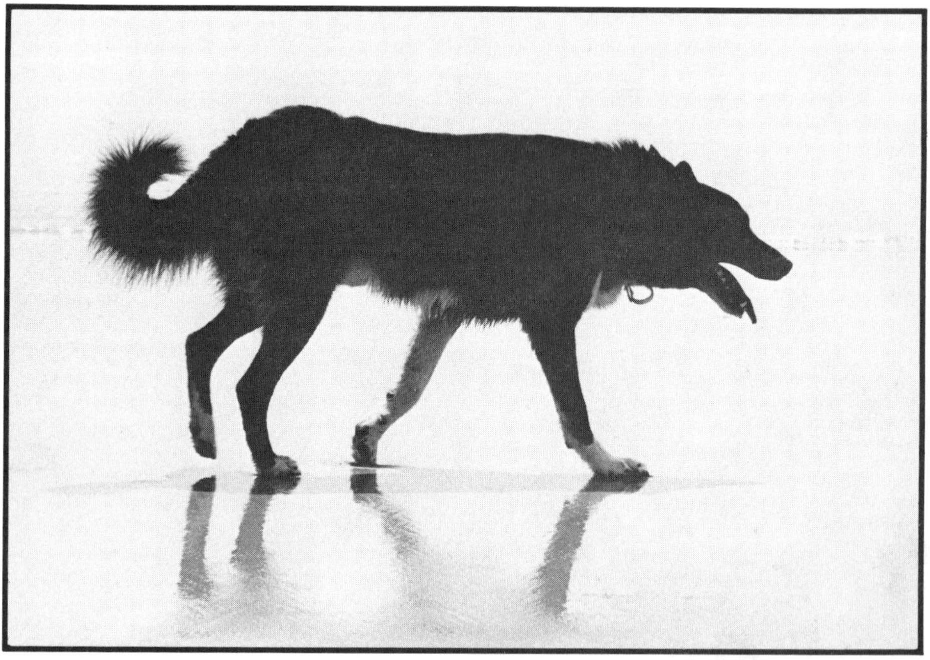

WATCHDOG

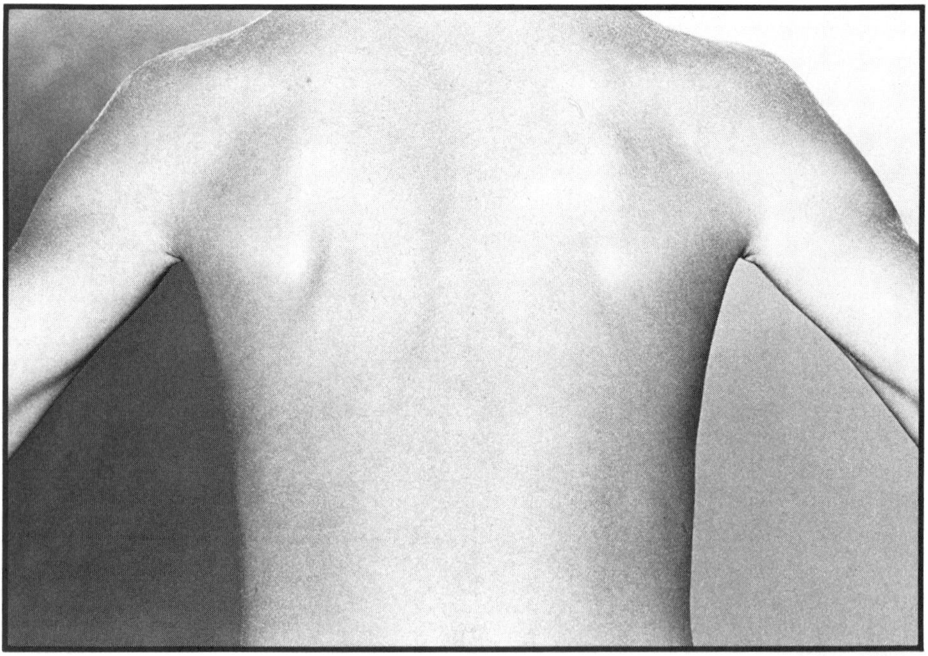

PIGGYBACK

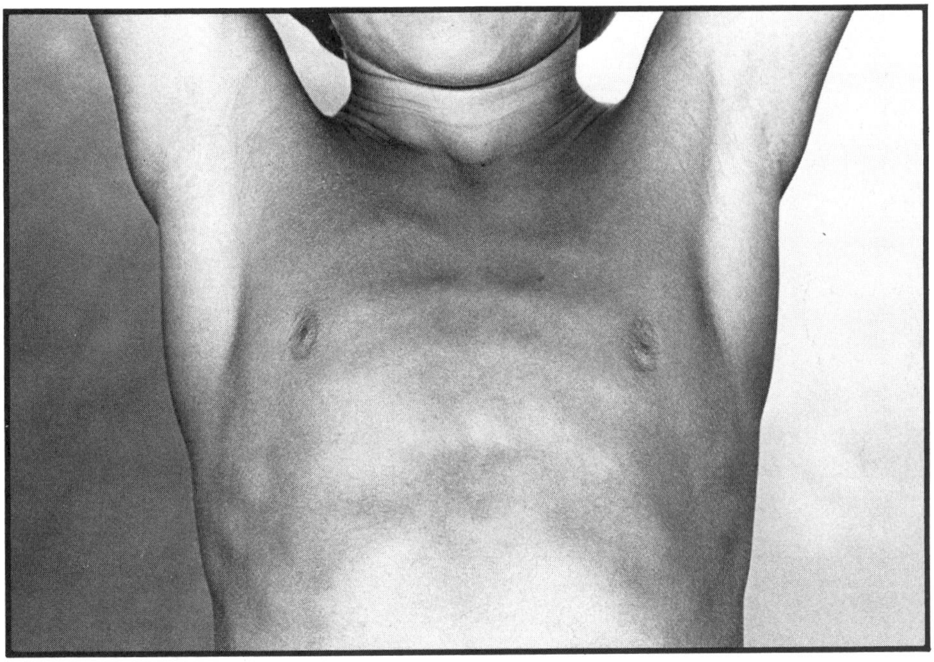

CHESTNUTS

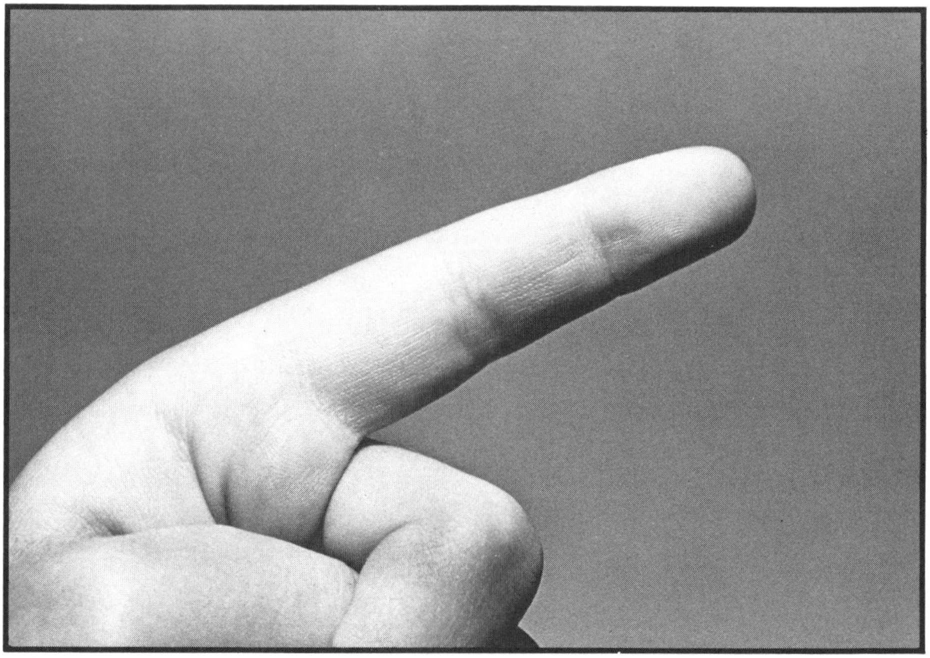

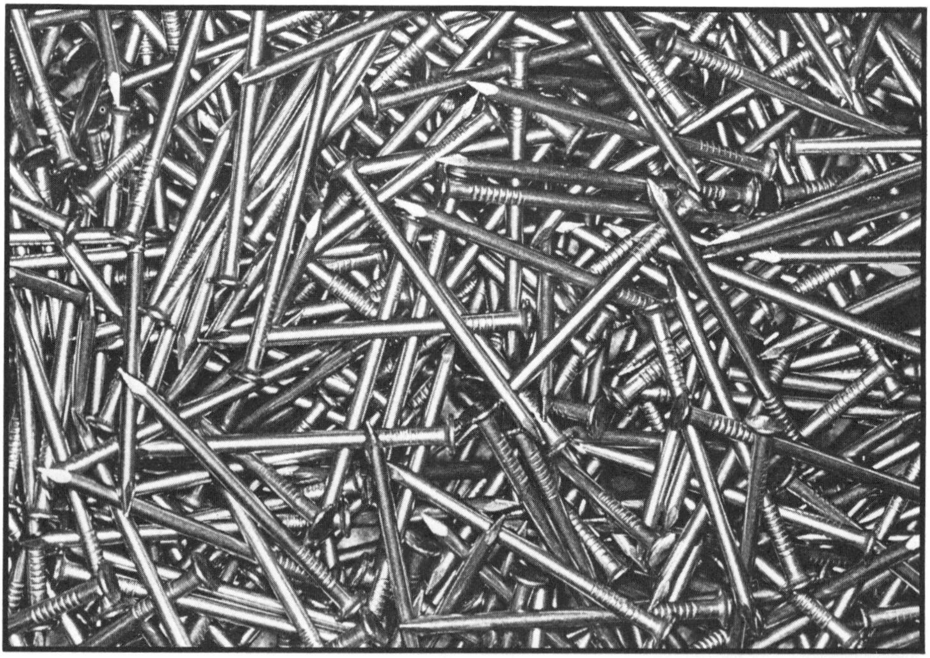

FINGERNAILS

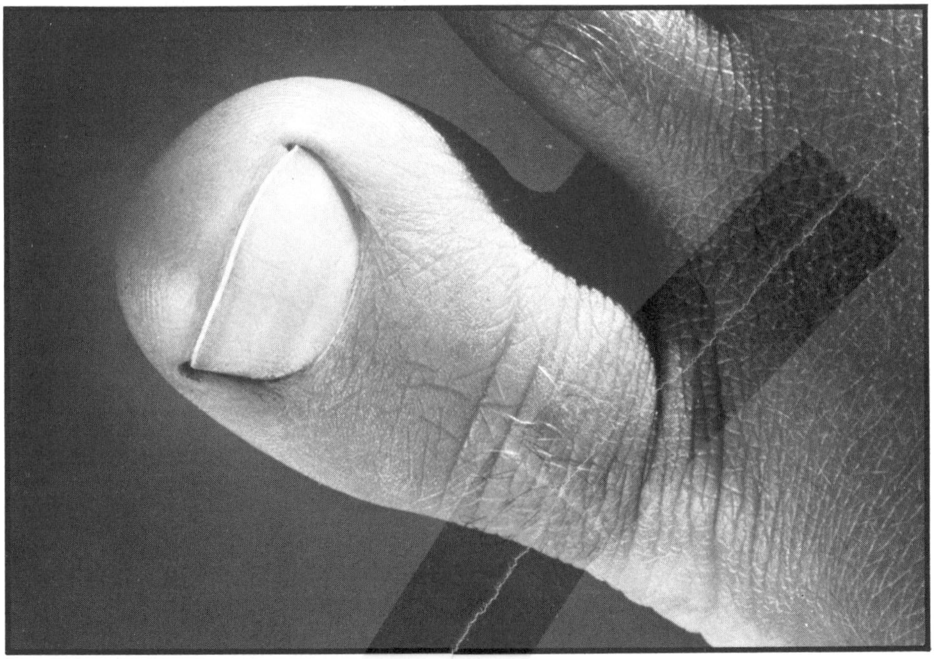

TOW TRUCKS

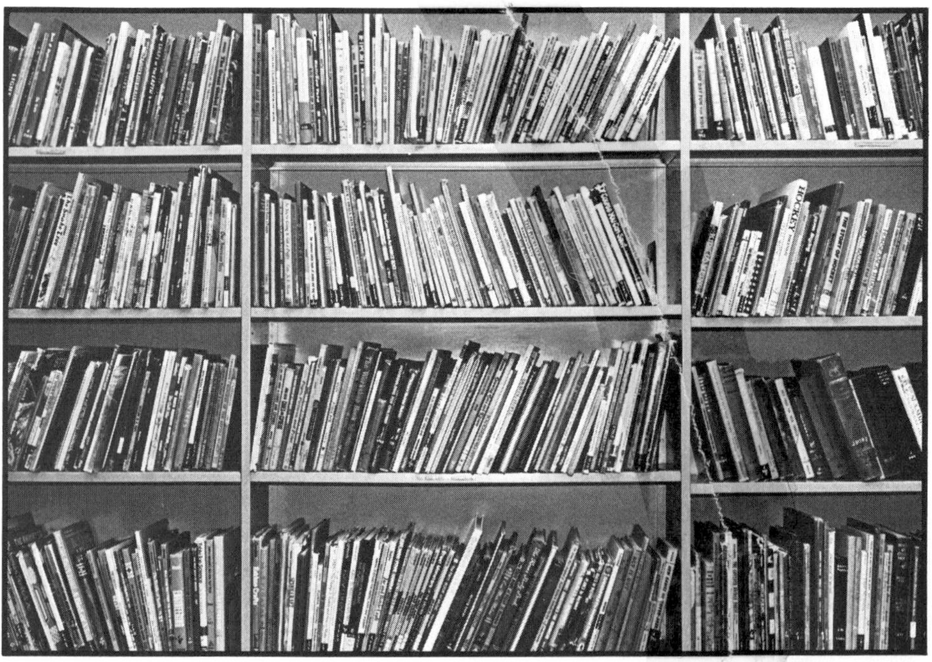

POCKETBOOKS

HAIRBRUSHES

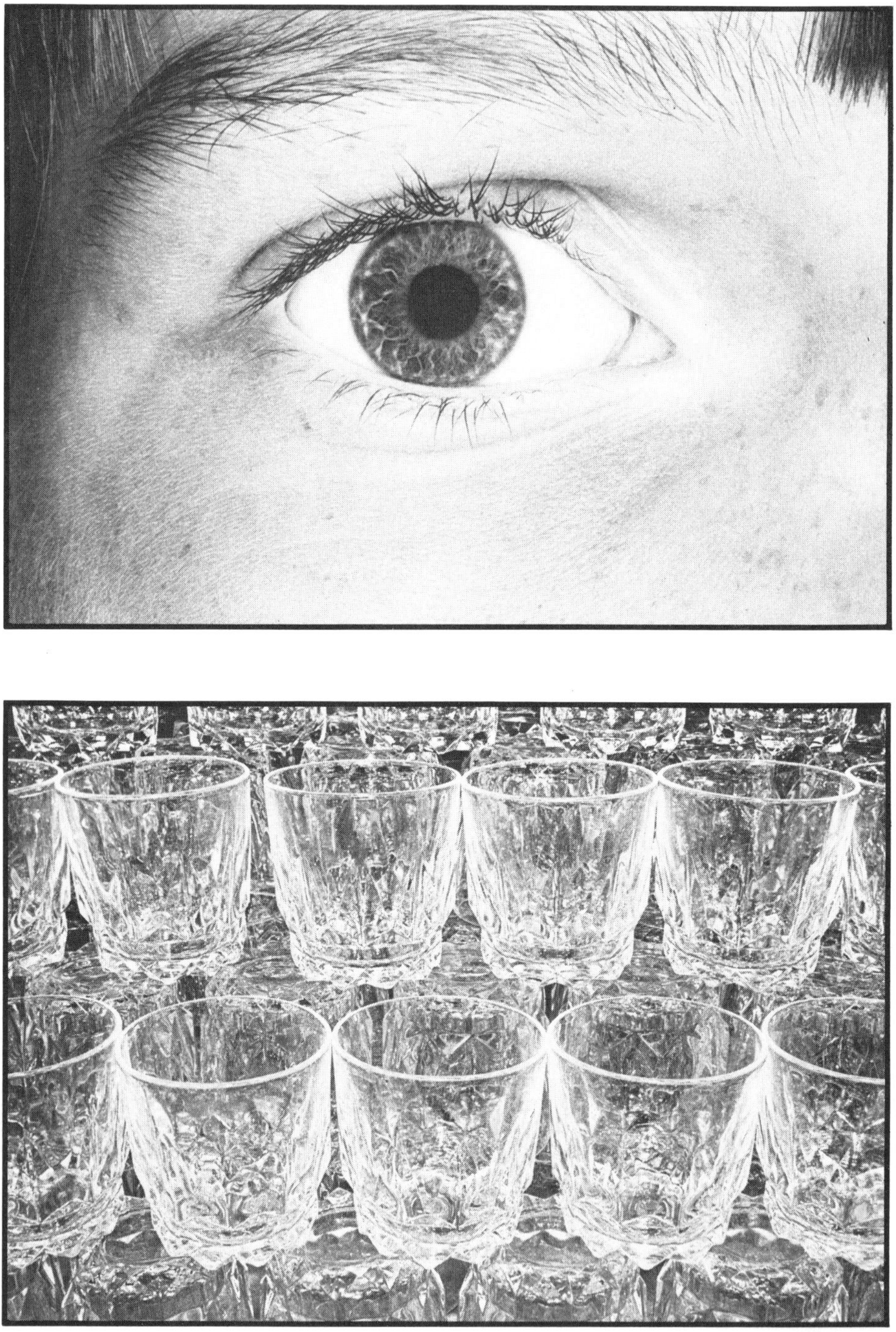

EYEGLASSES

COOKIES

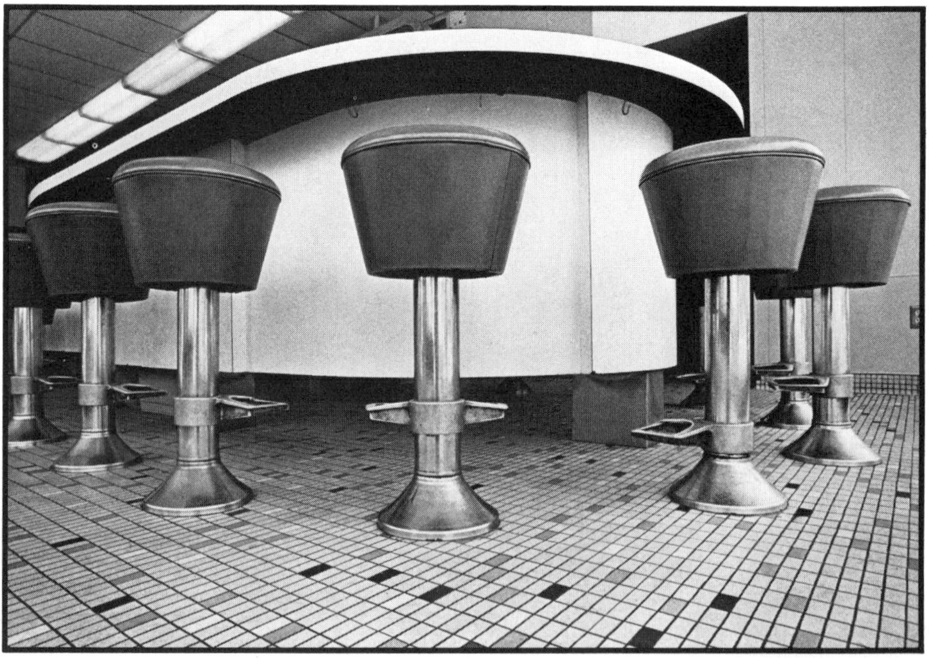

TOADSTOOLS

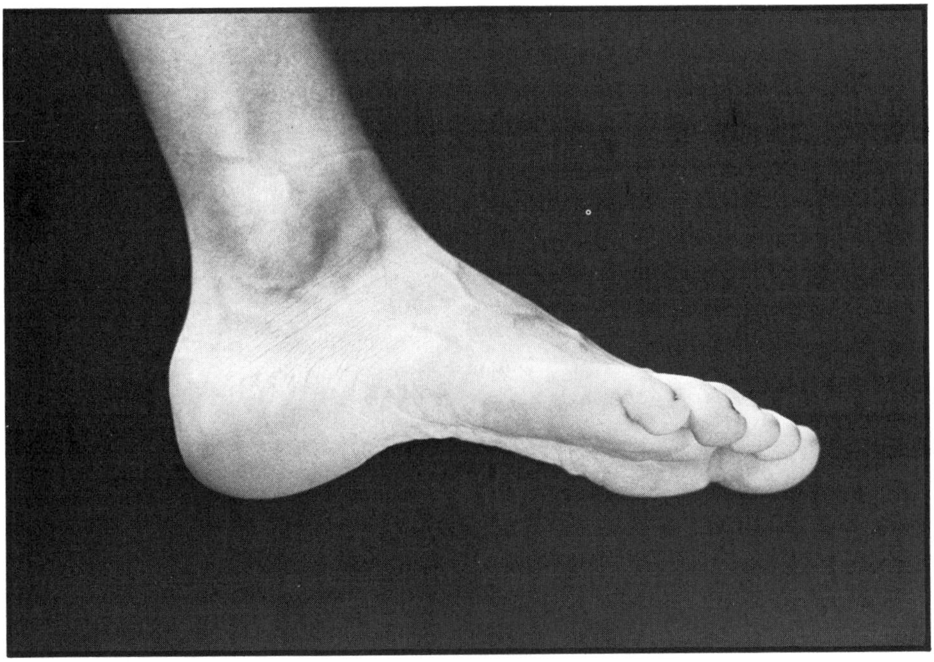

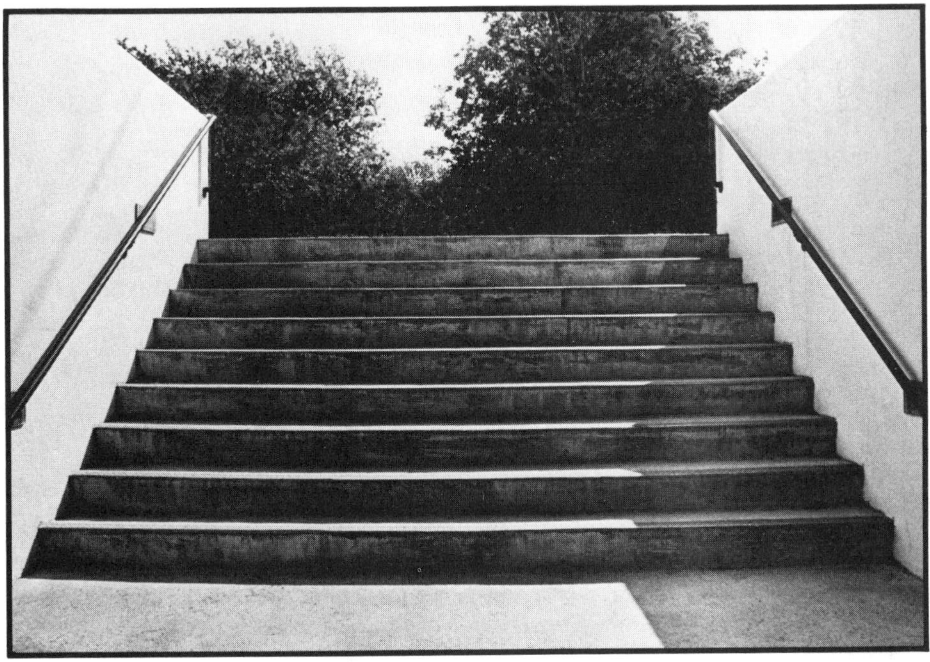

FOOTSTEPS

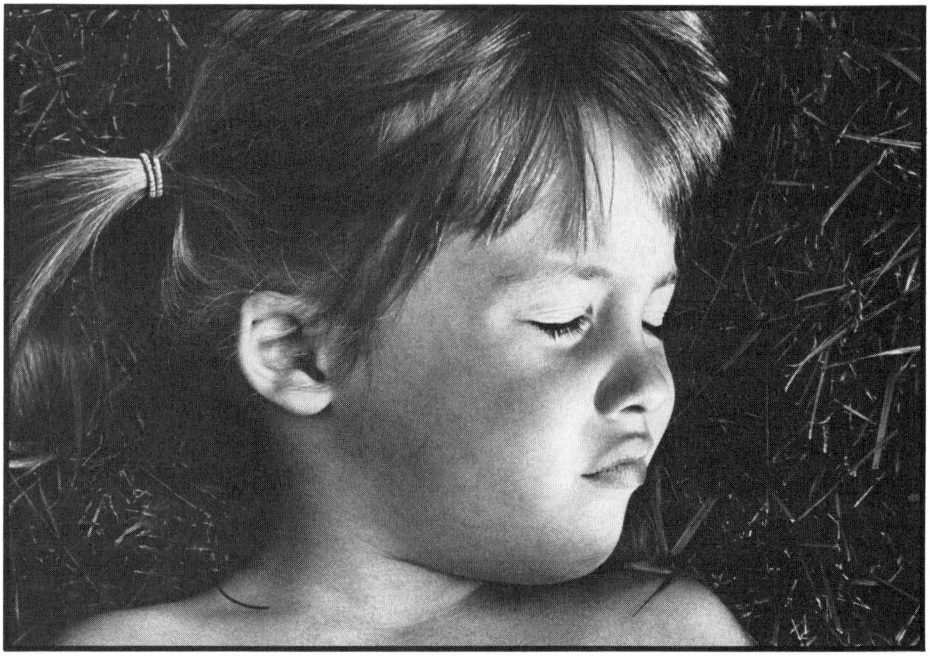

SLEEPING BAGS

CORNY

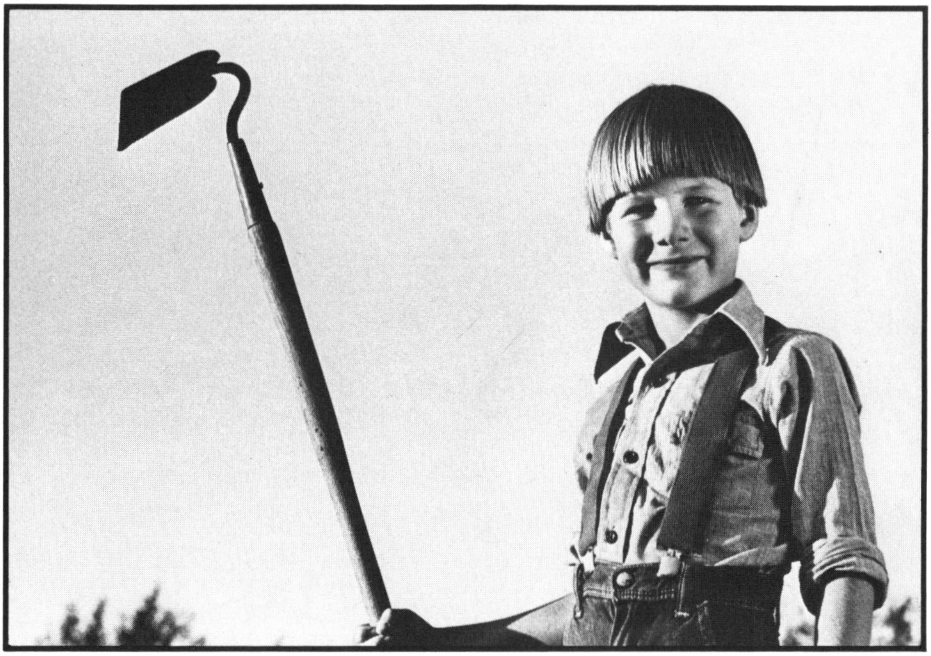

¡OH OH OH

Acknowledgments

For all their help and assistance while photographing *Puniddles,* many thanks to the following people, animals, and organizations:

York's Wild Kingdom Animal Forest and Amusement Park; "Regor" (cow) Ridley; Christopher Bland, Shawn LaFrance, Richard Goodwin, and Michael Bland; The Captain Lord Mansion; "Tammy" (dog) McMillan; John Tucker; (chicken) LaVigne and George LaVigne; Erin McDermott and her parents, Tom and "Kippy"; The Springvale Hardware Company, Inc.; McDougal's Orchards; "Dusty" (collie) Rivard and Linda Rivard; "Kahn" (dog) Remertsen and Kathy Remertsen; (pig) Miller and Walter "Bing" Miller; Albert R. LaValley, Inc.; Melissa Sargent; Carl Subler Trucking, Inc.; Brian Titcomb; The Springvale Public Library Association; (rabbit) Cann and Lawrence Cann; Roberta Pomeroy and The Clay Hill Farm; Dick Furness's Dunkin' Donuts; Jessica Massanari and her mother, Nancy; Joshua Mather and his parents, Barbara and Mort; Frank and Virginia McMillan; and number one photo assistant, Brett.